For Debra McClinton

© 2011 Cameron + Company
Photographs © Stephanie Rausser, www.stephanierausser.com
Doll by Jess Brown™, www.jessbrowndesign.com
Story by Nina Gruener
Edited by Amy Novesky, www.amynovesky.com
Book design by Sara Gillingham, www.saragillingham.com
Printed in China.   Third Printing

Library of Congress Control Number: 2011938102
ISBN: 978-0-918684-50-9

Cameron + Company
6 Petaluma Blvd. North, Suite B6
Petaluma, CA 94952
www.cameronbooks.com

Kiki
Coco
& in
paris

Photographs by Stephanie Rausser,
Doll by Jess Brown, Story by Nina Gruener

Coco belongs to a girl named Kiki.

When Kiki holds Coco's hand, Coco's feet skim the floor like a ballerina. It's as if they were made for each other.

Today they are busy packing for a trip to a city called Paris.

The airport is a maze. Coco has to be placed in a plastic box and sent through a tunnel. She doesn't like to be apart from her girl.

The flight is long as they cross the ocean, but they have each other to play with and the time passes quickly.

When they finally arrive they collapse into
soft sheets.

Kiki's feet twitch and Coco wonders what
her girl is dreaming about.

When Kiki awakes, they explore the flat where they are staying.

They have tea parties at a very high table.
They play hide-and-seek and stand on their heads.
They share secrets on a warm sunny deck.

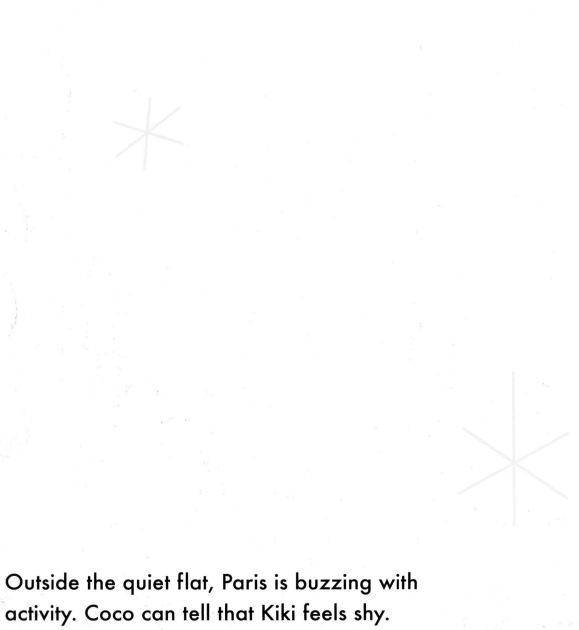

Outside the quiet flat, Paris is buzzing with activity. Coco can tell that Kiki feels shy.

Together, Kiki and Coco walk down bumpy little streets. They visit real palaces, and they try hard not to giggle in quiet museums.

Never apart from her girl, Coco is the luckiest doll in the world.

They ride a merry-go-round over and over till Kiki can't walk straight.

They sit atop a Ferris wheel, and they soar down an enormous slide.

Kiki squeals with delight and squeezes Coco's hand.

Next, they visit a Parisian salon.
Coco holds very still while Kiki puts
on a funny cape and sits in a big
chair. "Très chic!" someone shouts,
and they giggle to themselves.

Two little bobbed heads bounce
as Kiki skips to the one place they
haven't seen yet.

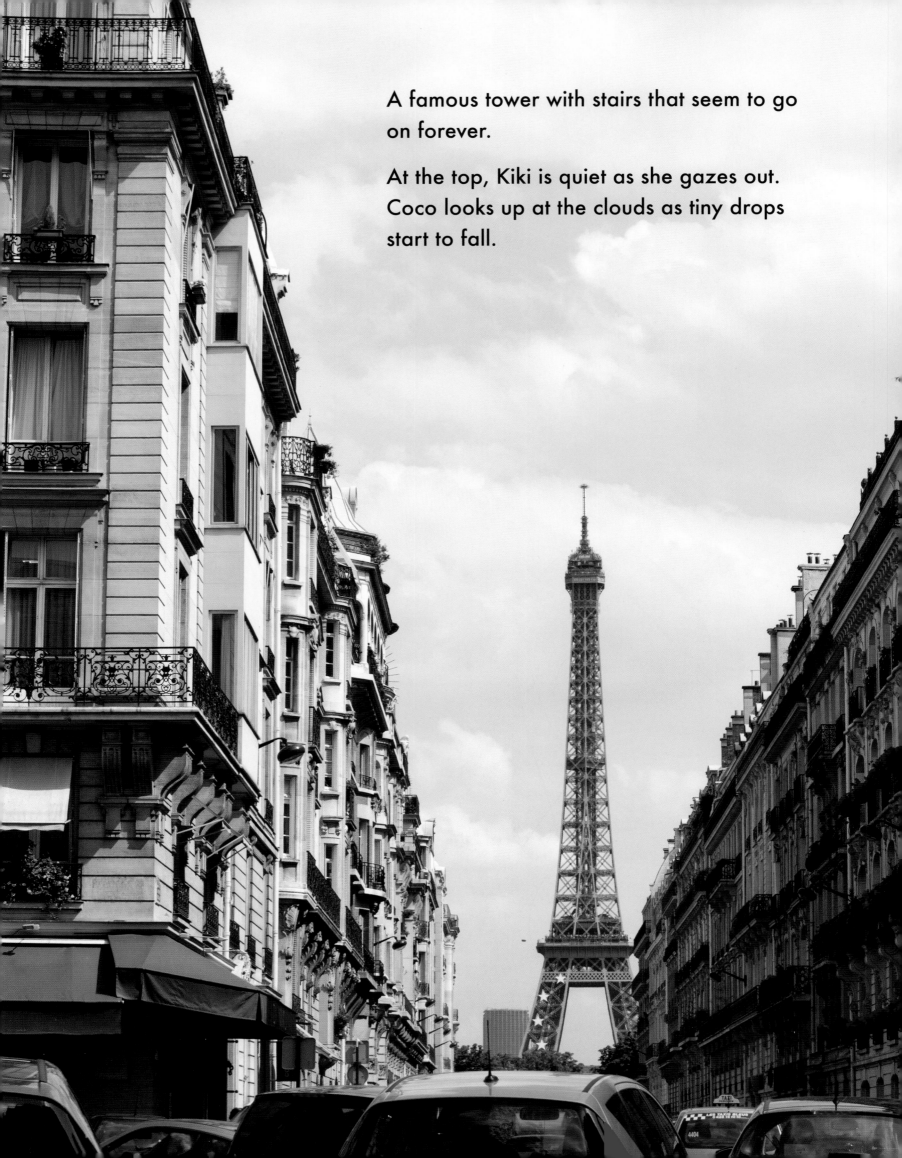

A famous tower with stairs that seem to go on forever.

At the top, Kiki is quiet as she gazes out. Coco looks up at the clouds as tiny drops start to fall.

Coco and Kiki are beat. They stop for a bite to eat at a busy café. Kiki nestles Coco next to her. But when she spills her drink, she flings Coco onto another chair to keep her from getting wet. Waiters rush this way and that. It is time to leave. In all the commotion...

Kiki forgets her doll.

Coco waits. Surely her girl will dash back in for her. The table is cleared and reset. Coco can't feel the sun on her muslin skin or hear the sounds of Paris without her girl. She is just a doll on a chair.

Suddenly a dark wet nose starts sniffing around her. And then she is moving, but her feet don't skim the ground like they should. Oh, where did her girl go?

Just when Coco thinks she will never twirl from
her girl's hand again, she hears the sweet sound
of Kiki's voice shouting her name. The dog drops
her. As she falls, her tiny button shoulder snaps...

The pitter-pat of little feet, and Kiki is above her.
She scoops Coco up off the cold ground and whispers
promises that she will never ever forget her again.

Kiki takes Coco to a special shop where dolls
like her are made.

The doll maker's hands move quickly as she
attaches the little arm with a brand-new button.
When she is placed back in Kiki's hands,
Coco's feet dangle just right.

A long soak in a big tub and Coco is as good as new. She does a few cartwheels to dry off.

That night Kiki and Coco gaze at the sparkling tower.
It seems to be lighting up just for them. Just as Paris was
made to sparkle, Kiki and Coco were made for each other.